Contents

D1377968

3

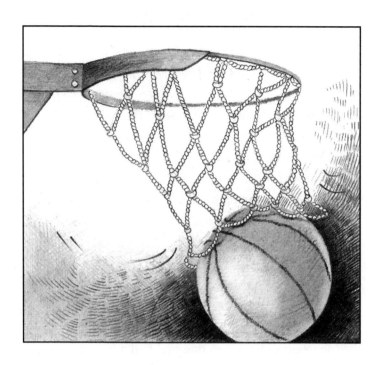

1

Nobody Cares

The bleachers shook as feet stomped and voices roared. There was no escaping the noise.

Jared Washington looked around at all the people. He knew he should feel proud. But all he felt was anger. He looked back at the court as the team in gold stole yet another pass. One gold player sprinted toward the other end of the gym.

The cheering began again. "Ni-na! Ni-na!"

People jumped to their feet as the player in gold went for the layup. Still seated, Jared watched as his older sister easily made the basket. He knew she would make it. She always did. Even when she played at home against their father.

The crowd was silenced by the loud buzzer. It was halftime. The home team, the Golden Bears, trailed the visitors by seven points.

Now Jared jumped to his feet. He grabbed some friends on his way down to the court.

"Hey, guys!" he called out. "Let's go shoot a couple."

Three boys from the crowd made their way down the bleachers. The tallest one grabbed a ball from a rack by the court. After a shot from outside, a game of two on two began.

There was no question about it. Jared was the best. He guarded his player well. He never let him get more than one or two steps ahead of him. With an occasional bump—all in fun—Jared stole the ball and took shots from anywhere and everywhere on the court. He couldn't miss.

After each shot, Jared would look up into the stands. But his parents weren't watching. They were just talking to someone else's parents. He wondered if he'd ever do anything that his parents would notice!

Again the buzzer sounded. Jared took one last shot from the half court line—a genuine swish! A few whistles came his way, and even some applause. But none from his parents.

Jared slumped his way back to his seat. His parents were still chatting with the others. Jared heard Nina's name mentioned.

In fact, *any* time he wasn't thinking about something else, he could hear Nina's name. And even when he *was* thinking about something else.

Nina really was awesome. And Jared knew it. She spent a lot of time teaching him some of her tricks.

For a while, all the colleges had been calling their house. And Nina had finally decided to go to State. Jared thought things might slow down after that—but, no! Nina was still the house hero—the local hero—the State hero! Jared couldn't believe it! He just got so sick of hearing about how *great* Nina was all the time.

There were only a couple of minutes left in the game. The Golden Bears were ahead by one. He really did want Nina's team to win. But he wondered if his parents would be as proud of Nina if her team didn't win.

Jared watched more intently with this thought in mind. With thirteen seconds left, the visitors stole the ball. One player made a baseball pass down the court. One of their forwards was waiting under the basket.

She plucked the ball out of the air and placed it gently against the backboard. The crowd fell silent as the ball fell through the net.

There were only seven seconds left. The Golden Bears were down by one. And all of their time-outs had been used.

Jared knew what would happen. But still he wondered what his parents would do if it didn't happen. It didn't matter.

The ball was passed inbounds. Instantly, the player made an outlet pass. Nina had already made her way down the court. The pass came, and she was able to catch it on the go. Her defender met her right at the top of the three-point line. Nina paused as though ready to fake her out.

But then, Nina suddenly pulled up for the outside shot. She made a slow, perfect motion. The buzzer sounded just as she released the ball. No one on the court or in the crowd made a move. It was like slow motion.

Jared's fingers were crossed. All eyes were on that ball as it slowly spiraled through the air. Nina's arm was still up in its follow-through position. Jared's eyes went up and up and up as they followed the ball. Then they closed.

Suddenly there was a burst of noise. Were they cheers or sighs? He opened his eyes.

Nina was being carried off the court by all her teammates. She'd won the game for her team.

Jared jumped up in excitement. But then he remembered. He'd wanted the Golden Bears to lose. Just to see what his parents would do. Oh, well. His thoughts were interrupted by a big hug from his father.

"That's quite a sister you've got, huh, J?" his father asked.

"Yeah, Dad, sure," Jared muttered.

"What say we go grab a bite to eat to celebrate?" his father offered. "Let's ask Nina what she wants."

Jared didn't say anything. He just followed his father and mother as they made their way down the bleachers.

Nina was surrounded by her friends. They were all laughing and drinking from their water bottles. Jared saw the coach walking toward them. And soon she was telling them how great Nina was!

What's new? Jared thought to himself. *Everybody* knows she's great. So why do they all keep telling us?

"Hey, Jared, what did you think?" Nina asked.

"You did it again," Jared said quietly.

"Yeah, but you know what?" Nina asked. "If you'd gotten the ball, you would have done it too!"

Jared looked up and smiled. Then he shook his head. He looked to see if his father had heard. But he and Mom were still talking to the coach.

"Yes, you would have," argued Nina. "I saw that shot you made right before the second half!"

"Yeah? Do you really . . . " Jared began.

"Hey, Nini," their father said. "How about celebrating with a visit to the land of banana splits?"

"Oooh, that sounds perfect, Dad," replied Nina. "Let me grab my stuff."

Jared was quiet as the family walked to the car. He just looked around. He saw Mom. He saw Dad. And he saw Nina. He wondered if any of them saw him. Well, he knew Nina did. But what about his parents?

What would happen, Jared wondered, if I just disappeared? Would they notice?

He knew that was a stupid thing to even think about. He was lucky to be a part of his family. And he was really lucky that Nina was his sister!

Everyone at school thought Nina was the coolest girl around. And he guessed that made him the coolest brother around.

But was that really enough?

That night, Jared lay in bed wondering what he could do. Nina was so good at basketball. He'd never be that good at anything.

Jared could shoot hoops, but that didn't make him a player. In baseball, he could catch any strike, foul ball, or ground ball that came his way. But he didn't want

10

to play baseball. He could even do well in school. But none of that seemed to be enough.

Slowly, Jared fell asleep.

In the morning, Jared's mother came to wake him up. Jared wondered if he'd even slept. He dragged himself out of bed and into the bathroom. He couldn't help staring in the mirror. He knew what to expect, and he knew what he saw. But how did others see him? How did his parents see him?

"Jared's a good boy." That's what his mother's friends always said. "What a nice boy!"

"Gee!" he said aloud. "A nice boy! Big deal! I'm sick of being nice. I want to be cool or awesome at sports. Or something!"

Inside, Jared knew he was a good kid. But somehow, it wasn't enough.

Then suddenly he had an idea. He saw his eyebrows go up in the mirror.

Who always got the attention? It didn't matter whether it was on the bus, in science class, at baseball practice, or anywhere. The same guys. It sure wasn't the Jareds or the other "nice boys." It wasn't even the Ninas. It was the guys who never listened. Or who talked while the coach was talking. Or launched spitballs around the bus. It was the "bad guys" who got the attention.

That's it! Jared thought. That was the way to make sure his parents would notice him. He'd just be bad! That must be pretty easy. And for that matter, it sounded fun.

Jared looked in the mirror one more time. It was the same face. But he thought he saw something different. He sure hoped so!

Jared ran down the stairs two at a time. He called to his mother, "I'm late, Mom. I'll see you later."

"Okay, hon," his mother cried. "Have fun at school!"

Ha! Jared thought. School! That's not in my plans. I'm off to do whatever I want. I don't care what I'm *supposed* to do. I've always done that, and it doesn't work!

With that thought, he set off. Where should I go? he wondered.

Jared turned down a street. He let himself just wander along. He saw the neighbor's dog running around. He watched the leaves dance in the breeze. He saw the traffic lights change. Once. Then twice. Then again.

Jared wandered some more, not really thinking about anything. That is, not until he suddenly found himself just where he did *not* want to be. He was right at the schoolyard gates!

He stared at the building and pictured himself in math class. He'd be copying down the problems from the board. Then he'd work them. He'd raise his hand with the answer. And he'd wonder how this was going to help in real life.

I wouldn't have to be doing all those things, he thought. Instead, I could be writing notes. Or crawling around underneath the desks tying people's shoes together. Or even better, throwing crumpled pieces of paper at the teacher's back. I could actually have a really good time and never have to worry about real life.

Jared laughed to himself. It did sound kind of fun. So he headed toward the entrance.

"You're late, Jared Washington," Mr. Wynn called out from the front of the classroom.

"So? Big deal," Jared heard himself say.

The other children looked at Jared in surprise.

"Excuse me, young man," Mr. Wynn said. "What did you just say?"

"I said, you're right. What about it?" Jared repeated.

"Why don't you walk out that door and start over?" demanded the teacher.

"Sure. Whatever you say," Jared snickered.

The other students watched Jared leave. They waited for him to come in, but the door never moved.

Jared tried to peer in. He wanted to see, or at least hear, what was being done and said.

"Let's continue," said the teacher as he made his way to the door. Jared turned quickly and ran.

Something inside Jared felt awful. He had never spoken to anyone like that in his entire life. But something else felt really good. He had done it! And he was sure his parents would be hearing about it.

But they didn't.

Once again, Jared went to sleep wondering what to do. Tomorrow was Saturday. He couldn't skip school. He'd have to think of something else to do to get a little attention.

2

Trouble

Jared woke up thinking about his game. He wished so much he could do something for his team. Like Nina had done for hers.

But baseball was different. There weren't any buzzers or last-minute three-pointers. Baseball was slow. And you had to rely on the other team to set up a play. Then, if it were the bottom of the ninth inning— with two outs and a tied game—maybe, just maybe, you could make an unbelievable catch that people would remember. Even if only for a couple of hours!

As Jared thought about this, he suddenly remembered something. He was supposed to be being *bad,* not good!

"I don't care about my game!" Jared said aloud. "Who cares if we win or lose? It's so stupid. The pros aren't even great. The only cool thing they do is spit brown gunk all the time!"

Even though Jared said this aloud, he knew better. He heard a little voice inside his head.

"What are you *thinking?*" the little voice asked. "You've always wanted to play catcher for the Phillies! Cut it out! Put on your uniform and get to the game!"

Jared was torn. He knew what was right. And he knew the little voice had said what he truly wanted to do. But then he thought about all the times he had done what everyone *else* wanted him to do! And where had that gotten him? Nowhere.

Slowly, Jared walked over to his closet. He leaned down and searched his laundry. His mother had asked him to fold it, but he hadn't. He just didn't care.

Finding his jersey and pants, Jared walked toward the bathroom. He knew he had to go the game. He had no choice. Plus, baseball was the only thing he really liked doing. It wasn't worth being bad if it spoiled the fun!

As Jared dressed, he watched his every move in the mirror. The little voice inside told him he looked pretty darned solid. He was a ballplayer his teammates could rely on.

Jared ate his breakfast. He told his mother what time the game began and then jumped on his bicycle.

When he got to the field, he saw that his whole team was already out playing. Jared panicked. He threw down his bike and ran toward the field. He looked toward the coach. And then he saw the look on his coach's face. Jared could feel his heart pounding.

What's going on? he wondered.

"Hey, Coach," Jared called. "I thought we were supposed to be here at nine-thirty. It's only nine-twenty!"

The coach looked at him and just shook his head.

"You know, Washington," the coach began. "I could see a lot of other guys doing this. But *you?* No! I really thought you had what it took to make it. Look at you!"

"What?" Jared moaned. "I'm on time, aren't I?"

"Who cares about time, Washington?" retorted the coach. "You are in the *wrong* uniform. Are you color blind or something? You're wearing white. Look out there. Do you see anyone else in white? Yeah—*the other team!*

"You're the starting catcher for *this* team," the coach continued. "And now you, all by yourself, have let this team down. The little Salter kid has been dying for this chance. And now, you know what? He's gonna get his big break—hand-delivered to him!"

"Coach, I swear, I didn't mean it," panted Jared. "I was hurrying to get here on time. And I mean, really, I was ready for this game—"

"Don't give me any of that," snarled the coach. "I watched you at practice the other day. You just kind of sulked around. You want to be a superstar. You just don't want to have to *work* for it!"

"That's not true," whined Jared. "I'll do anything. I'll get here early. I'll . . ."

But Jared suddenly stopped. He bit his lip. Who's saying these things? he asked himself. This is perfect. I couldn't be in this much trouble even if I tried.

Then he said aloud, "Whatever you say, Coach. I guess you're right; I don't care. Let the kid start."

The coach just grumbled under his breath.

"You let us down, Washington," the coach hollered. "Remember that!"

Jared slumped away. Inside, his heart was broken. He couldn't believe he had just quit so easily. On the other hand, he had done some major damage.

That coach really learned his lesson, he thought.

"You're being really stupid," said the little voice inside him. "You didn't do damage to anyone but yourself. Oh, and maybe the little Salter guy!"

Jared shook his head hard. "Cut it out!" he screamed. "Leave me alone. You don't know!"

"Yes, I do. And you know it," insisted the voice.

Jared's thoughts were interrupted by a loud cheer. He could see someone from the other team rounding second. He looked out at the outfield and saw Jonathan throwing hard to home plate.

Then Jared's eyes turned to the little tiny person dressed in all the padding. Even the catcher's mask was too big. Jared wondered how the Salter kid could see.

And then suddenly, Jared realized he probably couldn't see. The runner was heading home. The throw was on its way too. The catcher reached out to catch the ball just as the runner crossed the plate. The ball bounced off the catcher's chest into the mitt. But it popped out and fell to the ground.

The other team was now ahead by two. And the game wasn't even three minutes old!

"You blew it!" whispered the voice. "You really blew it!"

"Leave me alone!" Jared screamed as he ran away from the game. He ran and ran. He even ran by his bike, kicking a little dirt in its direction. But then he went back to get it. Slowly he climbed on it. And before he knew it, he was riding full speed.

Thirsty and frustrated, Jared finally slowed down. He couldn't believe he had gotten himself into this much trouble. He felt awful about his team. And he felt really awful for the little Salter kid.

He remembered back when all he had wanted was to start as catcher. But his coach had told him to be patient.

Tired and mad, Jared wandered into a grocery store. He was mad at everything and everyone. Nina for being so good. His parents for ignoring him. His coach for making him feel so bad. The little Salter guy for blowing it. And everyone else.

But Jared was really furious with himself. He'd made everything worse for everyone. And all just because he wanted his parents to pay as much attention to him as they did to Nina.

What a wimp I am, he thought as he reached onto the shelf to grab a soda.

"Uh, huh," echoed the voice.

Placing the can on the counter, he looked around the store.

A wimp? I'm not a wimp if I do something *really* bad, he thought to himself.

Slowly, Jared lowered his hand to the shelf just under the counter. Without even waiting for his change, he grabbed the soda from above and a pack of baseball cards from below.

He did it! He stole something! Now his heart was really beating.

Rushing out of the store, he ignored the calls from the man to get his thirty-five cents' worth of change. He didn't even notice the sign on the door saying "Shoplifters will pay for their crime." And last of all, he didn't see the small old man standing right in front of the door.

SMASH! Jared's head ran right into something. But then it gave way. He looked down on the ground. A man was lying on the sidewalk. He was smaller than Jared's grandmother. This guy was even smaller than the little Salter boy.

The old man didn't move. He didn't say anything. It didn't even look like he was breathing.

Jared's eyebrows went up. He bent down to see, but then he looked at his hands. There, right in front of him, was the pack of cards that he had stolen from the grocery store.

This is it! he thought. I'm going to get caught.

Jared looked back at the old man, then at the cards. And then behind him at the store. He saw the man from the store walking quickly toward him. From the other direction, he saw a lady in high heels coming toward him!

They were closing in on him. And he was going to get in more trouble than he had ever been in his entire life.

Scared, Jared jumped up. He looked down at the man one more time. For a second, he saw his grandmother.

"Stay, Jared. Make sure he's okay," advised the little voice.

Not a chance, thought Jared. This is more trouble than I could have ever wanted!

And then he ran off toward his bike. He rode and rode until he couldn't ride anymore. And then he rode a little more. And a little more until he saw his house. Looking over his shoulder one more time, he turned right up the driveway.

He was in for it now. That was for sure!

3

Guilty

Jared opened the door slowly and quietly. He poked his head around the door. Nobody there. He stepped inside.

Where is everyone? he wondered.

"Mom?" he called. Nothing.

So he tried again. "Dad? Nini? Anyone?" But no one answered.

"You're in for it now," whispered the little voice. "They've probably all gone down to the police station. You stole a pack of baseball cards. And what's worse, you left a poor old man lying on the ground. You're bad, Jared. Just plain bad."

Jared hated the voice. Everything it said was true. Sure, he'd wanted to be bad. But he hadn't wanted to hurt anyone. He'd thought that if he were bad, he would just get his parents to notice him. Now his parents would have to notice him in *jail!*

Suddenly, Jared could feel nothing but horror and anger. He had gone too far. He slammed the door. The windows shook a bit, and then everything was quiet.

Jared turned to go up the stairs when he heard his mother's voice.

"Hello?" his mother called. "Is everything all right? Who's there? Nina?"

"It's just me, Mom," Jared mumbled.

"Hello?" demanded his mother's voice from upstairs.

"It's just me!" screamed Jared. "I already said that!"

Mrs. Washington stood at the top of the staircase. She looked down at her son. She saw a sweaty young man in a baseball uniform at the bottom of the stairs. His pants were torn at the knee.

"What happened, darling?" Jared's mother asked. "Are you okay? How did you tear your pants? You look an absolute mess! Are you sick?"

Jared just stood there shaking his head. Then he looked down at his pants. He hadn't even noticed the rip. He must have ripped them when he ran out of the store and flattened the old man.

Jared stared at his mother, waiting for her to ask about the game. But she didn't say anything.

"Jared?" she asked. "Jared, are you listening to me?"

Jared wanted to scream. He wanted to ask her why she hadn't come to the game. Why didn't she or Dad ever come to his games? He wanted her to know that he'd worn the wrong uniform. He wanted her to know that he'd done something even he couldn't believe. He'd hurt someone. And he hadn't even stopped to make sure the man he'd hurt was okay.

Mom doesn't even care about the things I've done, he thought.

He wanted her to know he'd stolen the baseball cards. And even more, he wanted her to know that he was *glad* he'd stolen them! Now, he would get the attention he deserved.

Suddenly, his thoughts were interrupted. The phone was ringing. Jared's anger slowly melted into fear.

"That's probably the police," said the little voice inside Jared. "They figured out that *you* stole the cards and hurt the man. You know, you might have even killed him."

"Leave me alone," Jared said under his breath.

He watched as his mother walked toward the kitchen to answer the phone. He saw her looking back at him with worried eyes.

If she were really worried about me, Jared thought, she'd have come to my game.

He tried to listen to what his mother was saying. He couldn't tell if it was the police, or perhaps even the store owner. Or maybe it was the lady in the high-heeled shoes. He figured if it were any of them, his mother knew where to find him.

Jared ran up the stairs two at a time. He made his way to his bedroom and then into his bathroom. Again, he looked at himself in the mirror.

"And you looked so good this morning," said the voice. "You were going to make a difference to your team. You were going to play your best game. Now, look at you. You're a mess!"

And he was. Jared couldn't deny it. His face was dirty. His pants were torn. And his shirt looked as though a couple of guys had been playing tug-of-war with it!

He'd really messed up this time. His coach was furious. The old man was hurt. The store owner had been ripped off. His mother was worried. And he didn't even know where to begin to make things better.

The thrill he'd felt after stealing the cards was gone. The anger toward his mother was gone. The desire to be so bad was gone—because he *had* been bad! He'd been so bad that he'd hurt someone. He felt absolutely sick to his stomach.

Jared lay back on his bed, put his arms under his head, and stared at the ceiling. He saw the constellations he'd made with glow-in-the-dark stars. The stars had been a birthday gift. He thought back to his seventh birthday. And he remembered so many of the details.

His parents had taken him to a magic show. Jared had thought the magician was the greatest person ever.

Once again, Jared's thoughts were interrupted by the ring of the telephone. He wondered if *this* phone call was about what he'd done. He waited and waited, but his mother never came to get him.

Slowly his thoughts drifted off to different things.

He thought about the bad kids on the school bus. And then he thought about how well Nina played basketball. And then he thought about the little Salter guy. A feeling of sickness came over him again.

Jared rolled over and closed his eyes. When the phone rang again, he just pretended he couldn't hear it. Finally, he was able to block out everything around him. Maybe he would fall asleep. He hoped so. But then suddenly his eyes popped open.

What if . . . Jared thought. What if the man really *had* been killed?

He knew he hadn't hit the man that hard. But what if the man had had a heart attack or something. Jared couldn't think clearly. This was too much.

Without even thinking about it, Jared quickly changed his clothes. He threw his baseball uniform into the dirty laundry and headed downstairs.

"Mom," Jared called.

"Yes, honey," answered his mother. "I'm in the kitchen."

"Mom," he said slowly.

"Go ahead," said the little voice. "Tell her the truth."

"Mom," Jared said again. "I'm going for a bike ride. I'll be back in a little while."

"Okay, but wear your helmet," said his mother. "You don't seem to be thinking too straight these days. So I figured I'd just remind you."

"Yeah, sure, Mom." answered Jared. "I will."

Mrs. Washington watched out the kitchen window as Jared made his way to the garage. She knew something was bothering him. But she also knew her son. The best way to handle this one was to let him figure it out on his own. She had no idea what was running through his mind. But whatever he had done, she knew he could fix it.

She watched the front tire appear, and then Jared. She smiled to herself as she saw that he was wearing his black and white helmet. He had wanted that one so much. He'd said that all the big bikers were wearing that kind. She hadn't minded getting it. She thought it made him look like a little dog—like a cute little Dalmatian.

Sometimes when she looked at her thirteen-year-old son, she saw the five-year-old he'd once been.

With a serious look, Jared climbed onto his bicycle. He rode down the driveway. And just as he'd done so many times, he looked both ways before turning out onto the street. She watched him until he disappeared.

Jared rode along the street. He wondered if maybe he'd gone too far this time. Even though he wasn't in trouble with his parents or his teachers or really even his coach. He knew he was in bigger trouble than he'd ever been before.

Riding slowly, Jared pointed his bicycle back toward the store where he'd stolen the cards. The closer he got, the louder his heart was beating. Soon he felt out of breath.

"Calm down," said the voice. "You're doing the right thing."

For the first time, Jared was grateful for that voice. Before he knew it, he was at the store. There were little orange cones right where the man had fallen. Jared pictured the man's body in his mind.

Jared remembered the man clearly. He'd had white hair. He'd been wearing light brown pants and a blue shirt. The shirt had been tucked in and looked very neat. But the pants had gotten all muddy.

That must have been from the fall, Jared thought.

"Hey, kid!" someone called. "Watch where you're going!"

Jared realized he had biked right into one of the cones. He looked up to see who had been talking to him. It was the store owner. Jared panicked.

"Sorry, sir," he said with his head down. "I didn't mean to do that."

"No problem," smiled the man. "I just didn't want you to get hurt. These cones aren't usually here. It's just that we had an accident earlier today."

Jared looked up. The man didn't seem to recognize him.

"Really?" Jared asked in a scared voice. "Is everyone okay?"

"Well, son," said the man. "We're not sure. An old man got knocked down. And an ambulance had to come to get the poor guy. He didn't seem to be moving much. In fact, I'm not even sure if he was alive or not."

"W-w-well, what happened?" stammered Jared.

"Some little guy—a baseball player—was in a big hurry," replied the store owner. "He ran out of here like a crazy man or something. He didn't even wait for his change. Poor kid. He probably worked all summer for that money too."

Jared felt even worse after hearing the store owner say that!

"Anyway," the man continued. "The boy tore out of here and slammed right into the guy. I guess he got so scared he just ran. He seemed like a pretty good little guy—kind of like yourself. But he panicked! He was running and not watching where he was going. He's probably sitting around biting his nails right now. Anyway, they took the old guy to some hospital. Hope he's okay."

"You know what hospital?" Jared asked.

"Nah. What do you care anyway?" asked the store owner.

"Just wondering," mumbled Jared.

"Probably one of the ones downtown," offered the man.

"Yeah, probably," said Jared. "Anyway, sorry again for running into the cone."

"Not a problem, young man. You just take care of yourself," said the man. Then he added with a smile, "And make sure *you* don't go running down any little old men!"

"Right," called Jared as he rode off.

That night, Jared was quiet during dinner. He knew his parents were watching him. They'd look at each other and then at him.

Nina was out with some friends. So the quiet seemed louder than any noise Jared had ever heard.

"Everything okay, J?" asked his father.

"Yeah, Dad. Fine," replied Jared.

"Anything you want to talk about?" added his mother.

"Nah. Just thinking about some of the homework I have to do. You mind if I go up to do it now?" he asked.

"No, you go on ahead," answered his mother.

Slowly, Jared got up from the table. He picked up his plate and took it into the kitchen. He could hear his parents talking quietly. But he couldn't hear the words. All he knew was that they'd die if they knew what he'd done. And he knew *he'd* die if he didn't find out what had happened to the old man.

As Jared walked into his room, he felt the panic again. There on his bed were the baseball cards!

Why did I steal them? he asked himself. Those dumb cards.

He hadn't even opened them yet! And already, they had caused him more fear and problems than he'd ever had.

Jared picked up the cards and threw them in the trash can. Then he walked right over and plucked them back out. His mother would definitely wonder why he'd thrown away an unopened pack of cards. He just wanted them somewhere where they couldn't haunt him. He looked around his room. And then he just threw them under the bed.

But it didn't matter that the cards were hidden because he still saw them. He saw the cards. He saw the store owner. He saw the old man. He saw his coach. He saw his mother looking at him. And then his father. No matter how hard he tried, he saw everything he was trying to block out.

When the sun finally rose the next morning, Jared knew exactly what he had to do. And this time, he'd better do it right! No more wrong uniform, mouthing off at the teacher, stealing from stores, or knocking down old people.

Jared dressed in his regular school clothes. When he got downstairs, Nina was already eating breakfast.

"Hey, J," Nina said. "How're you doing? Didn't see you much this weekend!"

"I'm fine. You going on the bus today?" Jared asked.

"Nah, Sarah's picking me up," Nina replied. "She just got her license, and I'm the only one brave enough to go with her. I'd ask you to come, but I think that would make her nervous."

"That's all right," assured Jared. "I told Dan I'd meet him on the bus anyway. Thanks, though."

"Sure. See you at school then," said Nina.

A few minutes later, Nina and Jared left for school. Nina walked to the end of the driveway. And Jared walked toward the end of the street. He walked slowly. Soon, he saw Nina and Sally. They waved at him as they drove by.

As soon as they were out of sight, Jared ran back toward his house. He hid behind the big oak tree. No one could see him.

Jared watched as the bus rounded the corner. He was close enough to see the bus driver look toward Jared's house. But when the driver didn't see anyone, she just kept going.

Now Jared had missed the bus. And now he knew what he had to do. He walked toward his house.

4

He's Alive!

Jared kept his eyes on the garage door as he slowly neared the house. He had gone this far. And he certainly didn't plan on getting caught now.

He crouched behind the bushes and waited. His mother would be heading to work soon. He felt strange. His mother had always been the one to watch him. Now he was watching her.

The back door opened. Jared saw his mother walk out as she buttoned up her jacket. She was looking down at her hands as she searched for the keys in her purse. Suddenly, she lifted her head and looked right at him.

Jared's heart stopped. He was sure that his mother was staring straight at him. But she didn't say anything. She glanced around one more time and then headed toward the car.

Whew! That was close! Jared thought to himself. As his mother walked to the garage, he pushed back farther into the bushes. He wanted to be able to see her as she left. But he also wanted to make sure *she* didn't see *him!*

As Jared waited, he looked up at the sky. He began to think about the day ahead of him. Though he worried about skipping school again, he knew it was what he *had* to do! And as soon as his mother turned left, he was going to have to go to work fast. Really fast!

Finally, Jared heard the roar of the engine. He watched the taillights heading toward him as his mother backed out of the garage.

Jared ducked his head down farther without losing sight of the car. He kept his eyes on it until it backed into the street. Then it moved forward and out of sight.

Jared jumped up and ran to the front door. He leaned down and felt for the key under the doormat. He quickly unlocked the door, put back the key, and rushed in. He dropped all of his things—backpack, jacket, and baseball cap! Then he made his way to the kitchen. There he spotted exactly what he was looking for. The phone book.

Jared tore open the big book. He immediately turned to the yellow pages. At last he found the word *hospital*.

There was a whole page of hospitals listed. He'd never find out where the old man had gone.

Jared decided he needed a plan. First, he'd check out the addresses. Then he'd see which hospitals were closest to his side of town. Then he'd call each of those hospitals and see if the old man was there. If that didn't work, then he'd have to figure out something else!

Jared picked up the phone book, the phone, and a pad of paper. He walked over to the kitchen table. He needed to spread everything out. Then he could mark which of the hospitals he had called. And which of them had patients matching the old man's description.

Jared was nervous making the first call.

"Uh," he stuttered when someone answered his first call. "I was wondering if you could tell me something. Was an old man brought in to your hospital yesterday morning?"

The woman at the other end asked him many questions. So he finally hung up. He needed to sound like he knew what he was talking about.

Jared called another number. This time he was a little better. But the operator said that no older patients had come in by ambulance.

Jared called another hospital. And then another. And then another. No luck.

Then finally one operator said, "Yes, an older man was brought in by ambulance yesterday. He was run down in the street. But, I'm sorry to say, he passed away during the night."

Jared felt his hand begin to shake. He had trouble holding onto the receiver. The phone began to fall from his hand. But he could hear the voice saying something. He felt as though he were in a dream.

"I'm sorry," he mumbled. "What did you say?" He couldn't believe it. The worst had happened.

"Are you the boy who was with him when it happened?" the lady asked. "The doctor said that everything you did helped him to live a little longer. If you hadn't stayed with him when that biker knocked him down . . . "

"Did you say biker?" demanded Jared. "Was he hit by someone on a bike?"

"Well, no," said the lady. "It was someone on a motorcycle! But didn't you know that? Who *is* this?"

This time Jared did hang up! He hadn't killed *that* man. He looked down at his hand. It was still shaking!

"You keep calling, Jared Washington!" said the little voice.

Jared knew he should. And so he did.

Jared made three more calls. But he still hadn't found the old man.

There were only two more hospitals on Jared's list. He dialed the first one. Jared was hardly listening when the operator answered his question. Then suddenly he realized what the man was saying.

"Yes, son," the operator said. "An elderly gentleman was indeed brought in here on Saturday. He'd been knocked down on the street. And the person who knocked him down fled the scene. It's very sad. And I'm sorry to say . . ."

Again Jared's heart stopped. *This* was the man! And Jared was the one who had fled the scene. And now, the man was sorry to say—what?

" . . . and I'm sorry to say," he continued, "that no one has come to visit him. Are you his son?"

"Uh, no," stammered Jared. "But, um, well—I guess I'd really like to see him. Can I do that?"

"You bet!" assured the man on the phone. "Come on down. He's on the seventh floor, room 711. He'll sure be glad to see you!"

"I'm coming," Jared said quietly. "I guess I'll be right there."

Jared slowly hung up the phone. Now he was even *more* scared. He was glad to find out the old man wasn't dead. But he wasn't too excited to tell the old man that he was the one who knocked him down.

"You'll feel so much better as soon as you do it," said the little voice.

As usual, Jared knew the voice was right.

"Okay," he said as he took a deep breath. "I'm going."

The hospital was far away. So Jared figured he'd better ride his bike. He made sure he had his wallet and that the front door was locked. Then he put on his helmet.

At first, he rode slowly. But then he began to feel better about what he was doing. He rode faster and faster.

Jared was on his way to set everything straight. After today, he wouldn't have to think about any of this ever again. Or at least, that was what he hoped.

That was his last thought before he turned up the driveway to the hospital.

Jared rolled his front tire up next to a pole and then locked his bike. He sure hoped it would be there when he got back. If not, he'd have to call his parents to come and get him. He didn't know how he'd explain things if that happened.

The big revolving door kept turning, even when no one was in it. Jared timed it so he could just walk right in without ever having to slow down.

Once inside, he had no problem finding the elevator. The seventh floor had already been pushed. Everyone in the elevator was quiet. Jared was so scared, he couldn't even think.

What would he say? Should he have brought candy or flowers or something? Then he realized this was his first time in a hospital. First time, he thought. At least since I was born. And for a second, he smiled.

The elevator stopped and the doors opened. Jared saw a big number seven painted on the wall. He got out and looked around.

Jared saw a sign with room numbers and arrows on it. He began walking in the direction of room 711.

There it was! The door was only slightly open. Jared pushed it gently, hoping that maybe it wouldn't open. But it did. At least it didn't creak.

Jared could see the small outline of a body in the bed. The person's back was to him. And he saw gray hairs poking out from underneath a bandage.

The bandage made him feel sick! If it weren't for him, this man would not be here. And he sure wouldn't have some big bandage wrapped around his head!

Jared slowly circled to the other side of the bed. He didn't know what to expect. He hoped the man's eyes would be closed. And they were. That made him feel better. But the little tube coming out of the man's nose made him feel worse all over again!

Jared felt kind of weak. He turned around to lean on something and saw a chair. Though his back was turned to the old man, Jared could hear him moving! His heart jumped.

"It's okay," said his little voice. "Everything you're doing is good. Hang in there."

Scared, Jared turned around. The man's eyes were still closed. But now, he was lying on his back. With a deep breath, Jared moved closer to the bed. And then he began talking.

"I—I—I'm sorry," he whispered. "I would never have done anything to hurt you. Never. I've never hurt anyone like this before. I wish it hadn't happened. I wish you felt fine. And that you could be at home with your family. I'll bet they're all so scared that you might die. You won't die, Mister, you won't!"

Jared couldn't stop talking. Now he was talking about the little Salter boy. And his own family too! About how much he loved Nina and thought she was the greatest sister ever. About the baseball cards at the store. And he even heard himself saying how lucky he was to have his mother and father as parents. As he said the words, he knew they were true. But he wasn't sure where in the world they had come from.

"You *are* lucky," said the little voice.

Then Jared realized he already felt so much better. He reached out behind him to grab the chair. He sat down and breathed a sigh of relief. He leaned back and rested his head on the back of the chair, staring at the ceiling.

"I'm so sorry," Jared whispered. "Please know I'll never, *ever* do anything like that again. If there's anything I can do, I'll . . . " And then he stopped.

Suddenly, he realized what he had done. He had skipped school, made some phone calls, come to the hospital, and apologized all in one big blur. He had really done it!

"You did the right thing, young man," said a voice. Jared smiled. And then he closed his eyes. But then he opened them wide. Some*one* had said that. Not some little voice in his head.

"Excuse me," he said aloud.

"You did the right thing," the voice said again.

With a start, Jared brought his head down. Two big brown eyes greeted him. The old man was awake!

Immediately, Jared's heart began to race. He stuttered, "Oh, oh, my gosh. You're awake. Do you know who I am? Did you hear what I said? You must really hate . . . "

"Stop!" interrupted the man. "Slow down. Yes, I know who you are. And no, not one part of me hates you! In fact, a huge part of me is very impressed. Not many young men your age would have come and found me. You give me hope!"

"I—I do?" choked Jared. He stood up slowly and looked toward the door.

"In fact, you remind me of myself when I was a boy. But I think you might be smarter than I was," said the old man. "And if you *are* like me, I'll bet you want to run as fast as you can out that door. Am I right?"

Jared nodded slowly, never blinking his eyes.

"Well," continued the old man. "I'm going to make one request of you. Please don't leave. At least, not just yet! Won't you stay and chat with me?"

Jared stayed, but he knew that was probably stupid. Now the man was going to yell at him and tell him what a terrible boy he was. But that didn't happen!

"I want to tell you a little story I once heard," the old man said. "It's a story I think you will understand. Maybe even better than anyone else who's ever heard it.

"It's the story of a young man whose parents loved him a lot. But they just didn't know how to show it. When the boy was bad, they never bothered to sit down and talk to him. They just screamed at him and told him he should have known better.

"The young man figured they were right. His parents seemed always to be right. But one day, he was screamed at one too many times. His feelings were more hurt than he knew how to handle. So he left. He packed a bag of clothes and a little bit of food. Then he walked out the door.

"That was the last time he saw his parents. He thought he was being pretty brave. And perhaps he was. But life is a lot bigger when there's no bed or bathroom. No pats on the back good night. And no friends to shoot baskets with."

Jared kept his eyes on the man in the bed.

The man's voice became quieter as he continued the tale. "Soon," he said, "the young man found himself plucking things out of garbage cans. He was sad and he was lonely. He often asked himself if he had made a good decision.

"But just when he thought he should go back home, he met someone. He met an older man. A man who taught him the excitement of being independent. And the rewards of being responsible. That man taught the boy how to make it on his own."

After those words, the man closed his eyes.

"Are you okay?" Jared asked jumping up. He gently touched the man's hand. "Are you okay?" he whispered again.

"Yes, just a little tired," the old man replied. "That's the most I've talked in days."

"Then sleep," said Jared softly. "You need your strength to feel better."

"You're right, young man. By the way, what's your name?"

"Jared. Jared Washington," said Jared reaching out his right hand.

"Nice to meet you, Jared Washington," smiled the old man. "I'm Edward Bert. But they call me Ned."

"Mr. Bert," said Jared, "I'd better go and leave you alone."

"Perhaps you should," said Mr. Bert. "But won't you come back? I've enjoyed your visit."

"Yeah," Jared muttered. "I guess I could do that." But inside, he wondered if he would. He was afraid that Mr. Bert was just tired and that was why he wasn't angry. If Jared came back, that would give the old man another chance to scream at him.

"Yeah, Mr. Bert, I could try to come back," Jared repeated.

"Oh, that would be so nice," said Mr. Bert. "Really, would you do that?"

"Sure, why not?" said Jared.

"Well, then. Until we next meet," said Mr. Bert. "You're a nice boy, Jared Washington."

Jared walked toward the door slowly.

"You're nice too, Mr. Bert," Jared said.

He turned around and stared at the small man lying in the bed.

"Bye," called Jared as he walked out the door. He drifted toward the elevator. He wondered if it would be another thirteen years before he visited a hospital again.

Maybe. But then again—maybe not!

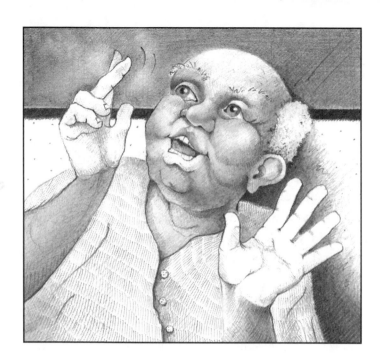

5

Like Magic

At home, Jared looked around at his family. He tried to see them through the eyes of the old man. Did his parents know how to show love?

Jared's feelings sure got hurt a lot. And lately they had been hurt even more. Maybe the old man had told him that story because he thought Jared should run away.

But then Jared looked around again. He liked sitting at the dinner table with his family. He liked knowing that his parents would come into his room at night. That they'd say good night. He liked—

"*Jared!*" called his father. "Are you listening to me?"

"Yeah, yeah. Sorry, Dad. What is it?" Jared asked. But he knew what it was. The school had called. They had told Mom and Dad that he'd skipped school again.

"I asked if you could please pass the salt," his father said smiling.

"Sure, Dad. No prob," Jared said with a relieved sigh. He wondered if they knew he'd skipped school. He was sure the school would call them. And it wasn't like his parents not to say something about it.

"You okay, honey?" asked his mother.

"Fine, Mom," Jared answered. Suddenly his thoughts went to the answering machine. Maybe the school had left a message. "Can I be excused, Mom? I'm feeling kind of tired."

"Aren't you hungry, J?" asked his father. "What's on your mind?"

"Nothing, Dad, I swear," replied Jared. "I just kind of want to get going on my homework. Then I can go to bed earlier tonight."

"Okay, then," said his father. "Go ahead!"

"Thanks, Dad," called Jared.

Jared went straight into the family room and looked at the answering machine. No blinking light. No message from school. He didn't know if he should be relieved or what.

Now, every time the phone rang, Jared would think it was the school. Or even the old man. Why had he told the old man his real name?

"Stupid!" Jared called himself. But he knew it wasn't really true. He'd done the right thing by going to see the old man. But now that it was over, it was time to get his act together.

Jared lay down on his bed. He stared at the ceiling. His thoughts went back to the ceiling in the hospital room. He saw the white walls, the white sheets, and the tubes in the old man's nose. But then he saw the sparkle in the man's eyes. And the wrinkles in his cheeks when he smiled.

Jared thought it was weird that a stranger knew more about his life than his own parents. He felt sick thinking about the many secrets he'd kept from his parents. He hadn't even been able to eat dinner with them.

Now, what was he supposed to do? It wasn't as though he'd done something really good that deserved lots of attention. He'd just done something okay to make up for something really bad that he'd done.

Lying on his bed, Jared wondered if he should tell his parents. He wondered if he should go back to the hospital. He wondered if he should go to school the next day. He wondered if maybe he should think about running away. Like the boy in the old man's story. He wondered what had happened to that boy.

The next day, Jared woke up thinking. He thought about the same things he'd worried about the night before. Nothing felt better. And none of the answers seemed to come to him.

So Jared did what he always did. He got up, brushed his teeth, and got dressed. Then he ate breakfast and walked to the bus stop.

As he sat on the bus, he looked around. These were the same people that had been on the bus last week. But they looked different somehow. They seemed younger.

"Sit down, right now, Joey Blaine. If I've told you once, I've told you a thousand times—*sit down!*" screamed the bus driver.

Jared began to think that it was true. That the bad kids always got more attention than the good ones. He watched as the bus driver screamed at another kid, and then another one. It made Jared feel strange to think that this is what he'd wanted to happen to him!

Slowly, Jared walked to his classroom. When he walked into the room, he looked around. He felt ashamed after what he'd said to the teacher. But none of the other children even noticed him at first.

"Hey, Jared!" called out one of the boys in his class. "Where you been?"

"Home," mumbled Jared.

"You sick or something?" asked the boy.

"Nah. I just needed to stay home," said Jared.

"Yeah, whatever," nodded the boy.

Jared waited. He knew someone would say something about his outburst in class. But no one said anything.

"Quiet, please. Everyone, please sit down," called out Mr. Wynn. He slowly closed the door behind him.

Jared watched the teacher's eyes look around the room. They fell on Jared and then moved on. Had his teacher forgotten? Jared wondered. He wished the teacher would just yell at him and be done with it. Instead, Mr. Wynn walked up to the front of the room. He took roll and then began the lesson!

Jared was so worried he couldn't think about the lesson. He figured the teacher would just ask to see him after class. But when the bell rang, Mr. Wynn said, "Class dismissed."

Jared got up with the rest of his classmates. He headed toward the door.

"Uh, excuse me," called Mr. Wynn.

I knew it, Jared thought. He stopped dead in his tracks. But when he turned around, Mr. Wynn wasn't looking at him. Instead he was handing a book to Jennifer Whipple. She'd dropped it.

Jared watched. He wondered if he'd ever be able to learn again. He couldn't think about anything except how rude he'd been.

Before he knew it, Jared's feet were leading him toward the teacher.

"Uh, Mr. Wynn?" Jared mumbled.

"Yes, Jared," said the teacher.

"I just wanted to say sorry for what I said the other day," said Jared with his head down. "I shouldn't have done that."

"Jared, I'm glad you said something," said Mr. Wynn. "I was surprised when you did it. And I guess I still am. But I also believe you must've had some reason for behaving so strangely. Did your parents tell you I called?"

"Uh, no, sir. They didn't," Jared said with surprise.

"Well, I asked them not to," said Mr. Wynn. "I was hoping you'd do exactly what you've done— apologize on your own. They should be very proud of you, Jared. They've taught you right from wrong! There is no lesson in life more important than that! Thank you for saying something. Now, let's forget it ever happened."

And with that, the teacher stuck out his hand. Jared reached out and shook it.

"Okay with me, Mr. Wynn," Jared said with a smile.

"Well then, see you tomorrow, Jared," said the teacher.

"Yup, see you then!" called out Jared.

Finally, it was the end of the school day. Jared didn't even think about what he had to do or where he had to go. Mr. Wynn had told him how proud his parents should be of him. And maybe they were. If they weren't, wouldn't they have gotten angry at him for talking back to the teacher? Jared thought about this the whole way to the hospital.

"Hello, young man," said Mr. Bert. "I'm so pleased to see you. I was hoping you'd come back!" He paused as he tried to sit up in bed.

"Let me help," offered Jared. He reached and grabbed Mr. Bert's hand. Then he helped arrange the pillows behind Mr. Bert. Jared was surprised to feel how strong the man was.

"I like you," continued the old man. "Even though you're the one who put me here."

Jared took a step back. Maybe it had been a mistake to come again.

"Don't be scared. I'm serious," said Mr. Bert with a smile. "I really do like you. And I may even like you *because* of this. Lying in this bed has made me feel happy for all that I have. I hope it's let you see how lucky *you* are to have all that you have!"

"Well, I don't know," said Jared. "What do you mean?"

"I mean that you aren't like that young man I was telling you about," answered Mr. Bert. "Do your parents scream at you? Do you want to run away from home?"

"No, I guess not. I mean, sometimes I wish my parents were different. But they aren't mean to me," said Jared. "What happened to that boy anyway?"

"Well, where was I when you had to go yesterday?" asked Mr. Bert.

"Some man was teaching him to make it on his own," said Jared.

"Oh, yes, I struggled. I mean, the *young man* struggled at first with the lessons," said Mr. Bert. "But finally, he was able to do what the man had taught him.

"First, he learned how to pull a coin from behind another person's ear." Mr. Bert continued. "This didn't earn him much money. But it was fun to do anyway. And plus, it seemed that the man liked the boy's company. Then he learned how to turn a coin into a dollar bill. Now things were beginning to happen!" exclaimed Mr. Bert.

"Before long, the two began to work together as a pair," Mr. Bert continued. "They traveled from town to town. They did their magic tricks on street corners. And sometimes they opened for bigger shows. One day, the younger man was supposed to meet his friend. But the man never showed up."

"What happened to him?" asked Jared. "What did the boy do?"

"Well, at first I went over to the man's house. And then I . . ." began Mr. Bert.

"Wait a second," said Jared. "What do you mean? Are *you* the boy in the story, Mr. Bert? Are you?"

Jared looked at the old man. Even without an answer, Jared knew the man in the bed was the boy in the story.

"Is this a true story? Or are you just teaching me a lesson?" Jared asked. He saw a look of pain in the old man's eyes.

"No, Jared. This is a real story," said Mr. Bert sadly. "This is *my* story. And I haven't told it to anyone in a long time. Remember the story you told me when you thought I was sleeping? I'll bet you haven't told anyone else. Am I right?"

Jared stared straight ahead. He couldn't believe he hadn't seen through Mr. Bert's story.

"Am I right?" repeated Mr. Bert.

"Yeah, you're right!" said Jared. "It's just that everything has been so much harder lately. I'm not really even sure what to think now!"

"Well, I'll tell you one thing to think about," advised Mr. Bert.

"What's that?" asked Jared.

"I want you to think about what you're doing tomorrow."

"Well, it's Saturday," said Jared. "I have a baseball game at 2:30. Other than that, not much. Oh, yeah, my sister has a basketball game tomorrow night. She only has two more before she graduates. I don't want to miss it!"

"Well, I can't say that I blame you," said Mr. Bert. "But I have a favor to ask you."

"Sure, anything, Mr. Bert," offered Jared.

"How about helping me escape from this place tomorrow morning?" asked the old man.

"*Escape?*" Jared cried.

"Well, not really. But they say I'm good enough to go now," said Mr. Bert. "And I don't want to stay in here any longer than I have to. What do you think?"

"Definitely!" answered Jared. "What time do you need me here? And, you know, I can't drive or anything!" Jared added.

"Oh, no, I'd just like some company as I head home," said Mr. Bert.

"Well, that I can do!" smiled Jared.

"Wonderful, just wonderful!" Mr. Bert said.

"Mr. Bert, can I ask you a question?" asked Jared.

"Of course, you may," answered the man.

"Are you ever sorry you ran away?"

The old man closed his eyes. Jared could tell he was thinking about what he'd asked.

"You know, Jared. Sometimes I am," Mr. Bert finally answered. "But then I find myself thinking about my life now. And I wonder if I could've gotten this far if I'd stayed. I'm sorry I left. But I think I would've been sorrier if I'd stayed. Does that make sense?"

Now it was Jared's turn to think. "Yeah, Mr. Bert, it does. I'll see you tomorrow!"

"Tomorrow it is then!"

Jared left the hospital. He knew how it felt to want to get away. But he knew even better how it felt to want to be home. And that's where he wanted to be now!

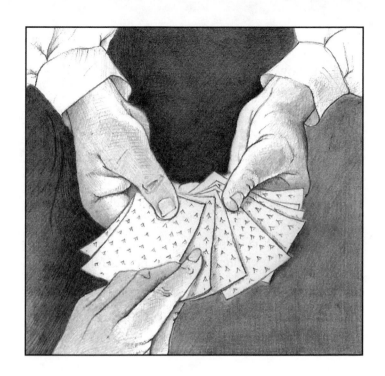

6

Abracadabra

Jared walked through the door of his house. He noticed the wonderful smell of his mother's meat loaf. He was happy to be home. And he wanted to tell his parents. As he walked toward the kitchen, he could hear their voices. Then he heard his name.

"I still don't think we should say anything to him," he heard his mother say.

"I'm not so sure of that," his father said. "He needs to know that you can't get away with skipping school. *And* talking back to your teachers!"

"He knows that!" insisted his mother. "And you *know* he does! Why else would he have apologized to Mr. Wynn?"

"Well, what exactly did he say to him? Did Mr. Wynn say?" asked his father.

Jared couldn't help listening to them. This was too much. They were talking about things he didn't even know they knew. He got up as close as he dared without making any noise.

"He just said that Jared had come up to him after class," said his mother. "And Jared said he was sorry for what he'd done. I don't know what else he said. But the bottom line is he knew he was wrong. And he was willing to do something about it."

"Well, if you really think that we should leave it as it is, I'll trust you," said Jared's father.

"Oh, Jordan," said Jared's mother. "You know him as well as I do! He's always been good. And he's always done the right thing. There's a part of me that's relieved that he was naughty for once. I have so much confidence in him. He knows the difference between right and wrong!"

"You're right," Jared's father said. "And Nina is always reminding us what a great little guy he is!"

Interrupting, his mother added, "And it's not as though she's an easy act to follow! He's just trying to figure out where he's going. I can't help but admit that even in these last weeks he's made me proud! It takes a lot of guts to apologize to a teacher. He's fine. I'm sure of it."

"You're right. Let's trust him on this one," his father added.

Jared tried to close his mouth. He couldn't believe all that his parents had said. They trusted him! They thought he had good judgment! *And* they were proud of him!

Even though he felt a little bad for listening to their conversation, he was glad that he'd done it! They were proud of him. And no one could take that away!

The next day, Jared couldn't wait to get to the hospital. He told Mr. Bert all that he'd heard his parents say.

When he finally stopped talking, Jared looked around. Mr. Bert had collected his belongings. He'd put them and the get-well cards he'd received into a plastic bag.

"Well, young man," he said. "I'm ready to go home!"

"You know, Mr. Bert. I don't even know where you live," Jared said.

"I live at the Pleasant Hollow Retirement Home," said Mr. Bert. "It's where older people live. So we can talk to people who remember things like Victrolas. Where people talk about the moving pictures. And how silly the idea of going into space is! It's where people live who are like me!

"I haven't lived there too long," Mr. Bert added. "And I can't say I liked it much *before* the accident. But I'm sure excited to get back there."

"What do you mean when you say it's where people like you live? I thought *we* were alike. Didn't you say that?" asked Jared.

"Yes, I did. And we *are,*" said Mr. Bert. "But you know what, young Mr. Washington? You are a whole lot smarter than I *ever* was! I wonder if I'd apologized for things, maybe my life would have turned out differently! No matter, now. Let's get going."

Jared picked up the small bag. And he and Mr. Bert set off to Pleasant Hollow.

When they walked through the door of the building, a tall, pretty woman came over quickly.

"Oh, Mr. Bert, we're so pleased to have you back!" the woman said. "How are you feeling? And who is this young friend?"

"I'm glad to be back, Sarah," answered Mr. Bert. "I didn't know how much I could miss this place filled with old people. So I thought I'd bring back a young person!"

Sarah laughed. "Well, he certainly looks like a nice young man!"

"Oh, that he is," smiled Mr. Bert, adding a quick wink in Jared's direction.

"Hey, this place is pretty nice, Mr. Bert!" exclaimed Jared.

"You ain't seen nothin' yet!" said Mr. Bert. "All those years of hard work finally paid off!"

"Oh, yeah. I want to hear the end of your story," said Jared.

"Later, Jared. Later," Mr. Bert said softly.

They made their way to the elevator. Mr. Bert pressed the seven button. And up they went. When the door opened, Jared saw a beautiful long hallway. There were doors on both sides of the hall. Mr. Bert marched down the hall to the last door on the left.

"This," he said as he turned the key in a lock, "is where I live."

He was so proud. Jared *knew* it would be wonderful.

Jared and Mr. Bert walked into the living room. Jared saw lots of pictures. He saw Mr. Bert meeting movie stars and presidents. There were photographs everywhere. He had been on the cover of *Time!* And all because of his magic tricks.

On the cover of one magazine, there was a picture of Mr. Bert and many children. The headline read,

"No matter how sad or hurt, a child feels better at the hands of Ned Bert!"

"Wow, Mr. Bert! You're famous!" cried Jared. "You know everyone."

"No, Jared, I don't know any of them," said Mr. Bert. "I've just been lucky enough to meet them. And I tried to make their lives better. You know, you could do that too."

"Do what?" asked Jared.

"You could learn some magic tricks and go around making people happier!" said Mr. Bert.

"You'd teach me? Really, Mr. Bert?" asked Jared. "That would be the coolest thing ever! Would you really do that?"

"Sure, I would. As long as you come and visit!" agreed Mr. Bert.

"I'll come every day!" shouted Jared.

And Jared did. Every day after school, he went to Pleasant Hollow and visited Mr. Bert. He learned new tricks. He met lots of people. And best of all, he went home each day knowing that he'd made somebody's life a little better.

Then one day, Jared went to the retirement home. There was no answer when Jared knocked on Mr. Bert's door.

Jared knocked again. And then he rang the bell. But still no answer. He glanced down the hall but saw no one.

Then Jared saw something on the floor. There was a note with his name on it. Jared picked it up and read it.

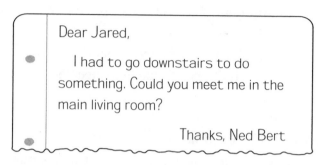

> Dear Jared,
>
> I had to go downstairs to do something. Could you meet me in the main living room?
>
> Thanks, Ned Bert

Jared felt a wonderful sense of relief. He stepped back into the elevator.

When he reached the living room, there were many people sitting on chairs and sofas. Mr. Bert was standing at the front of the room.

Before Jared had a chance to say anything, Mr. Bert spoke up. "And introducing the newest addition to the act, *Mr. Jared Washington!*"

Applause rang in Jared's ears. He walked toward the front of the room.

For twenty minutes, Jared and Mr. Bert performed magic. It was as though they'd practiced the show many times.

Mr. Bert found a rabbit underneath Jared's hat. And then Jared pulled an American flag out of Mr. Bert's pant leg. Back and forth they went—each doing something to the other.

They saved the trick Mr. Bert had learned as a child—turning the quarter into a ten-dollar bill—for their grand finale. And with the appearance of the bill, the room burst into loud clapping! Jared and Mr. Bert held hands and bowed as the crowd shouted, *"More! More!"*

Jared just smiled. And smiled. And smiled. He couldn't stop smiling.

He turned to Mr. Bert and whispered something in his ear. Now it was Mr. Bert's turn to smile.

With a strong handshake, the two performers left the room.

Jared went one way and Mr. Bert went the other.

It wasn't long before Jared was standing outside his own house. He peeked through the window. Nina was setting the table. His father was pouring milk. And his mother was getting out the plates. He heard his father yell.

"Jared? *Jared!*" he called. "Dinnertime! Please don't make your mother wait to serve the meal. It's getting cold."

Jared smiled. Then he raised his hand to the doorbell. He gave it three short pushes.

Within seconds, his mother was standing at the door. She stared at the two people at her door. At first, she looked confused. But then she slowly smiled.

"Hello! Won't you two come in?" she asked.

Jared smiled at her. He knew she could tell this was important to him.

Mr. Washington and Nina looked up from the dining room table. They saw two people wearing black coats, white shirts, and black pants. They recognized Jared. But they'd never seen the other person before. He was an old man!

Just then, Jared spoke. "The Magician Tradition," announced Jared. And with that, they began to perform their entire act. This time, though, the finale was a little different. Jared did it all on his own!

Reaching deep into his pockets, he pulled out a pack of cards. He glanced in Mr. Bert's direction. Mr. Bert gave him a quick wink and an encouraging smile.

"Mom," Jared said holding out the pack of cards. "Pick a card, any card."

Mrs. Washington reached out, stroked the pack, and carefully stuck two of her fingers between the cards. Slowly, she pulled out one card.

"Turn it over. And please look at it carefully," instructed Jared.

His mother followed the directions perfectly.

"Now, please, make sure not to let anyone see it!"

Again Mrs. Washington did as she was told.

"Now, I am going to place this deck of cards on the table. Please put your card *anywhere* in the deck. And please, Mom, remember what your card was."

His mother smiled. "Oh, I don't think this is a card I could very easily forget."

"Shhh!" laughed Jared. "Please, no hints." Then he whispered, "This is the first time I've ever done this trick."

His mother smiled back at him. Jared knew she was proud of him.

Jared divided the stack into five groups. And then six. And then two. Then Jared narrowed down his choice to four cards. They all remained face down. Picking them up carefully, he counted them. Then he shuffled them. And then, with lots of energy, he cried, *"Abracadabra! Here is your card!"*

He turned over the card.

"Is this it, Mom?" he asked.

"Yes, it certainly is!" his mother said with surprise. "How could I ever forget that card?"

The card was a picture of Jared, Nina, and their parents!

Everyone laughed. And then Jared introduced Mr. Bert to his family.

"Mr. Bert," Mrs. Washington said. "I don't know much about you except you've made my son very proud. I hope you'll stay and have dinner with us!"

"I'd love that," said Mr. Bert. "And I thank you for thinking that I made your son proud. But it is your son who has made himself proud. And I imagine he has made *you* very proud!"

WHAT'S THE TRICK?

Without a moment's hesitation, Jared heard a "definitely" from Nina's direction. Then a "he certainly has" from his mother's and father's directions. They *were* proud of him.

7

The Magician Tradition

The next morning, Jared woke up later than usual.
He felt the warmth from the sun shining into his
bedroom. He knew nothing could upset him today!

Jared and Mr. Bert had told his parents what had
happened. How Jared had run down poor Mr. Bert.
And then how he'd felt so guilty. How he'd gone to the
hospital. And then wondered if he'd ever go back.
They'd told them everything. Well—just about
everything.

Jared had told his parents about skipping school.
But they'd already known that. He told them about
mouthing off at the teacher. But they'd already known
about that too! He even told them about wearing the
wrong jersey to his baseball game, even though he
hadn't meant to. But they didn't seem upset about
that! He really *had* told them just about everything.
Everything, that is, except stealing the baseball cards
from the store.

It was stealing the cards that had gotten him into all
the trouble. If he hadn't taken them, he wouldn't have
run over poor Mr. Bert. And if he hadn't run over Mr.
Bert, then he wouldn't have skipped school a second
time. But—he *had* stolen the cards.

Jared waited for the little voice to tell him what a
bad kid he was! But it didn't come. Then he realized
that he hadn't heard the little voice in quite some time.

When was the last time? he asked himself.

He thought and thought. Then he remembered
being in the old man's room and hearing something.
He'd thought it was the voice. But it wasn't. It had
been Mr. Bert's voice!

Jared smiled to himself. His friendship with Mr.
Bert had replaced the little voice. He didn't need the
little voice anymore to tell him what to do. He could
figure out the right thing to do on his own!

Without another moment's hesitation, he sat up in bed. There was something he needed to do. He jumped out of bed. He threw on his jeans and a Phillies baseball shirt. Heading out of the room, he grabbed his baseball cap from the doorknob.

As he ran down the stairs two at a time, he placed the cap on his head. He made sure the capital P was centered above his forehead! He was ready to finish up with this whole thing.

"Mom!" he called toward the kitchen. "I've got to run and do something. I'll be back in about an hour."

"What about breakfast?" Jared heard his mother call.

"Later," he shouted as he closed the door behind him.

Again Mrs. Washington looked out the window at her younger child. She had known he would figure it all out.

She waited to see his bicycle come out of the garage. And when it did, she smiled! There he was— her little magician. So grown up but still her little boy! Just as she and Jared's father had told Mr. Bert the night before, they were so proud of him.

Jared approached the store a little more slowly than he'd left his house. He knew he was doing the right thing. But he was scared. He had done something wrong. No one knew about it. And now he was going to tell *on himself!* Nothing about that made any sense. Even so, he didn't want to hear his little voice telling him he'd better do it!

Reaching into his pocket, he found what he was looking for. They were a little more wrinkled than they'd been a couple of weeks earlier. Jared was glad that he wouldn't have to look at them anymore.

As he neared the door to the store, he could see his reflection in the glass window. Noticing his Phillies shirt and cap, he felt a little surge of confidence. He could do this. And he would. He certainly knew he should.

Slowly, Jared pushed open the door. Glancing around the store, he searched for the familiar face. His mind wandered back to the day when he had biked down here looking for the old man. It was strange to think of him as the old man. Because now he was Mr. Bert. He was a friend.

Jared thought about what the store owner had said to him that day. He remembered it word for word.

"And make sure *you* don't go running down any old men!" the owner had said.

Jared had forced a laugh. He *had* been the one to run down the man. And now he had to confess.

"Hey there!" Jared heard in the middle of his thoughts.

He glanced around the store. Over near the paper towels, he could see the man's head.

"H—h—hi," stammered Jared.

"You look familiar, son. Do we know each other?" asked the man.

"Uh, well . . . " began Jared.

"Oh, yeah, you go to my son's school. Aren't you on his ball team?" asked the man.

"No, sir. I don't think so," Jared said. "I—um—well, I'm . . . "

"No, no. I know," interrupted the man in the store. "You were here the other day on your bicycle, weren't you?"

Jared suddenly felt relieved. He could do it.

"Yes! Yes, that's right! I was here. And I have something I need to tell you," said Jared.

With that, he thrust his hand into his pocket. He pulled out the pack of baseball cards.

"Uh, sir," Jared began. "I took these. I took these cards from your store. And I'm really sorry. I really am. I don't even know where to begin. After I took them, I got so scared that I ran out of your store. And then, before I even knew it, I had run over Mr. Bert. You know, the old man who got hurt right outside your store.

"Well, after that, I was even more scared. I ran home. I didn't even wait to find out if he was okay. I

felt so bad. I thought I could forget about it if I didn't
see him. But when I got home, there were the baseball
cards I had taken from your store. They kept
reminding me."

"Slow down, young man," said the store owner.
Though his tone of voice was stern, his eyes looked
friendly. Jared didn't know whether he was going to
be mean like his words or nice like his eyes.

"No, wait. I can't," interrupted Jared. "I felt so bad,
I came back here. You told me then you thought the
man was okay. You also told me I shouldn't run down
anyone because I looked like I was too nice! I guess
I'm not. Anyway, I finally found the man in a hospital.
I felt so bad, I wish you knew how sorry I am."

"Well, then," said the man with a serious face.
"What did you do then?"

Then Jared felt suddenly quite relaxed.

"Oh," he started. "I went to visit him every day.
And then I helped him get out of the hospital. And the
whole time that I was visiting him, he was teaching
me some really cool magic tricks."

Finally the man gave a little smile.

"Anyway," continued Jared, "last night we went to
my house and surprised my family with a magic show!
I felt so much better once my parents knew. I thought
everything was fine, but then . . . "

"But then *what?*" asked the store owner.

"But then I remembered the cards," Jared continued. "I felt bad all over again. So I wanted to bring them back. And I also wanted to do something to help you.

"Even though I don't play on the same team as your son, I heard on the bus that his birthday is coming. Some of his friends were talking about it. I was wondering if maybe I could perform a little magic show at his party. I mean—that is—if you are *having* a party for him."

"Well, to tell you the truth, Sammy's mother and I were just talking about his birthday party," said the store owner. "We were thinking about getting a clown. But I sure think a magic show would be just as wonderful. You're a good boy, son. What's your name anyway?"

"Jared. Jared Washington," Jared replied.

"Well, Jared, I can't say that I respect what you did with the cards," said the store owner. "But you sure earn my respect in all that you have done since. My name is Mike Scott. You should be proud of yourself."

"Nah, I should be ashamed," Jared admitted. "And I am. Now, I just want to make it go away."

"Then why don't you leave me your number," said Mike. "I'll call you when we set a date for Sammy's party. Will the old man be with you?"

"Mr. Bert? I sure hope so. We're a pair," added Jared.

"I'm glad to hear that. Now, what's your phone number?" asked Mike.

Jared picked up a piece of paper from the counter and wrote down his phone number.

"Mr. Scott," Jared said. "I really am sorry for what I did. And I also know I'll never do anything like that again. Thank-you for being so nice. I'm lucky."

"Perhaps you are lucky, Jared," said Mr. Scott. "But you also made yourself lucky. You took a bad situation and turned it into a good one."

"Thanks, Mr. Scott! I guess I'll see you in a few weeks at the party!" called Jared.

"You bet!" agreed Mr. Scott.

With that, Jared ran out the door just as he had a few weeks earlier. But this time, there was no one standing in his way as he left. He turned around once more to look at his reflection in the window. He knew his Phillies hat was good luck!

When Jared got home, his mother, father, and Nina were eating pancakes.

"I saved some for you, honey," called his mother.

"Thanks, Mom. They look great!" said Jared.

"Where you been?" Nina asked.

Jared took a deep breath and made his one last confession. He saw disappointment on the faces of his family. But he also saw pride when he told them what he had done this morning.

He could tell that his mother wanted to say something. But she knew he'd already learned his lesson. He watched as she opened her mouth.

"You did the right thing, Jared," she said. "I'm proud of you. Mr. Bert knows what he is talking about, doesn't he?"

Jared just smiled.

"Oh, yeah. Speaking of Mr. Bert," said Nina. "There are a few things I want to know about!"

"Like what?" asked Jared.

"Like how you did all those tricks last night!" Nina said. "Some of them I think I can figure out. But there were others I just couldn't."

"Well, I can tell you some, Nini. But I sure can't tell you all of them. That would make me a traitor to my profession," he said laughing.

"How about if you just tell me one?" Nina begged. Mr. and Mrs. Washington watched their children and smiled.

"Sure," offered Jared.

"All right," said Nina. "How did you know that Mom was going to pick the card that had the picture of us?"

"Yes, how *did* you know that?" asked Mr. and Mrs. Washington at the same time.

"Well," Jared began. "I'm sorry to say, but that is just one trick I can't tell you about."

"Oh, come on!" cried out his parents and sister.

"Nope," said Jared looking down at his lap. And then he smiled.

Jared thought about the special deck of cards Mr. Bert had made for him. On every card was a picture of his family. It was his favorite trick.

"Come on, Jared!" insisted his family.

"I can't," Jared stated.

"Well, why not?" demanded Nina.

"Because," said Jared. "To *not* tell is the magician tradition! And just in case you didn't know, *I* am a magician!"

Jared looked around. His parents were looking at him in the same way they looked at Nina after a basketball game. They were proud of him! And best of all, he was proud of himself!